Published 2007 by Concordia Publishing House
3558 S. Jefferson Avenue, St. Louis, MO 63118-3968
1-800-325-3040 • www.cph.org

Text © 2007 Dandi Daley Mackall
Illustrations © 2007 Concordia Publishing House

Manufactured in China

1 2 3 4 5 6 7 8 9 10   16 15 14 13 12 11 10 09 08 07

The LIGHT of CHRISTMAS

By Dandi Daley Mackall

Illustrated by John Walker

CONCORDIA PUBLISHING HOUSE · SAINT LOUIS

Why do we need lights that tangle?
Can't we just have bells that jangle?
Ornaments that sparkle spangle?
Why are there lights of Christmas?

It was long ago, when there was no light.

It was dark, dark, dark as the darkest night.

Then the Lord said, "Light!" and the world turned bright.

How we needed that light from heaven.

We got light to separate night from day,

And a sun shining down to warm our way,

Then a moon at night with its silvery ray.

We lived in the light from heaven.

But the earth grew cold with the people's sin.
    Such a sad, dark state that our world was in!
As the evil spread, then the light grew thin.
    We needed a Light from heaven.

So the Lord set loose with His holy plan:
"I will send My Son for the sins of man.
No one else can help, but I know He can.
The world needs the Light of Jesus."

Then the Lord sent Gabriel in a blinding light
To a girl named Mary on a quiet night:
"You will bear God's Son. He will make things right.
God is sending the Light of Jesus."

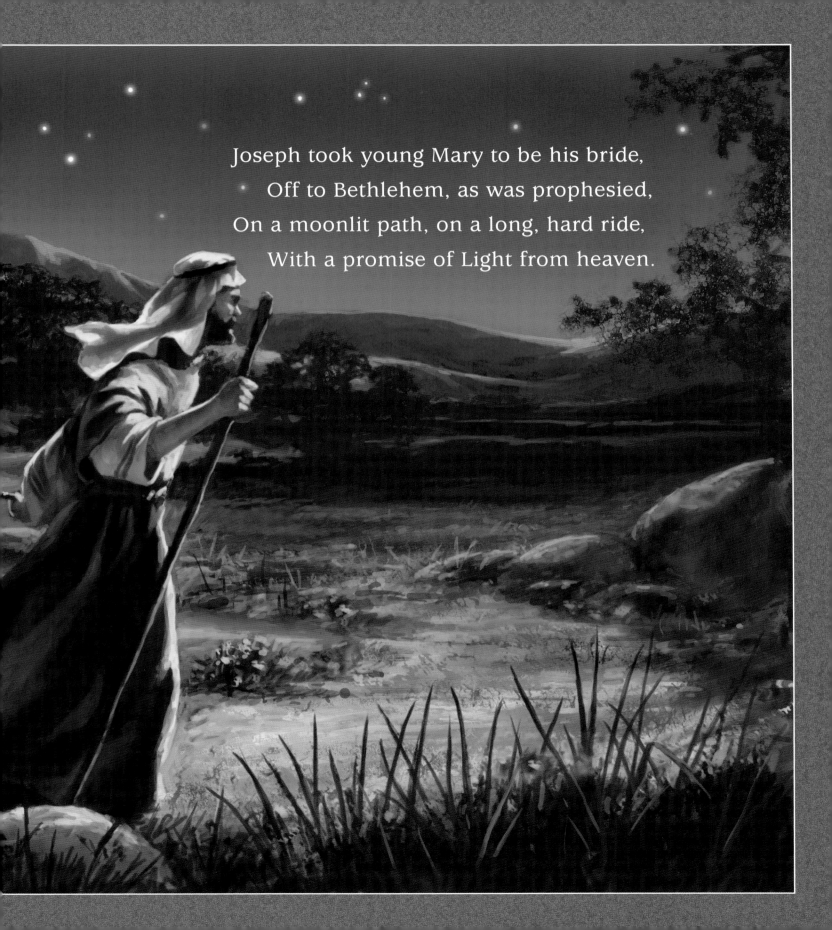

Joseph took young Mary to be his bride,
Off to Bethlehem, as was prophesied,
On a moonlit path, on a long, hard ride,
With a promise of Light from heaven.

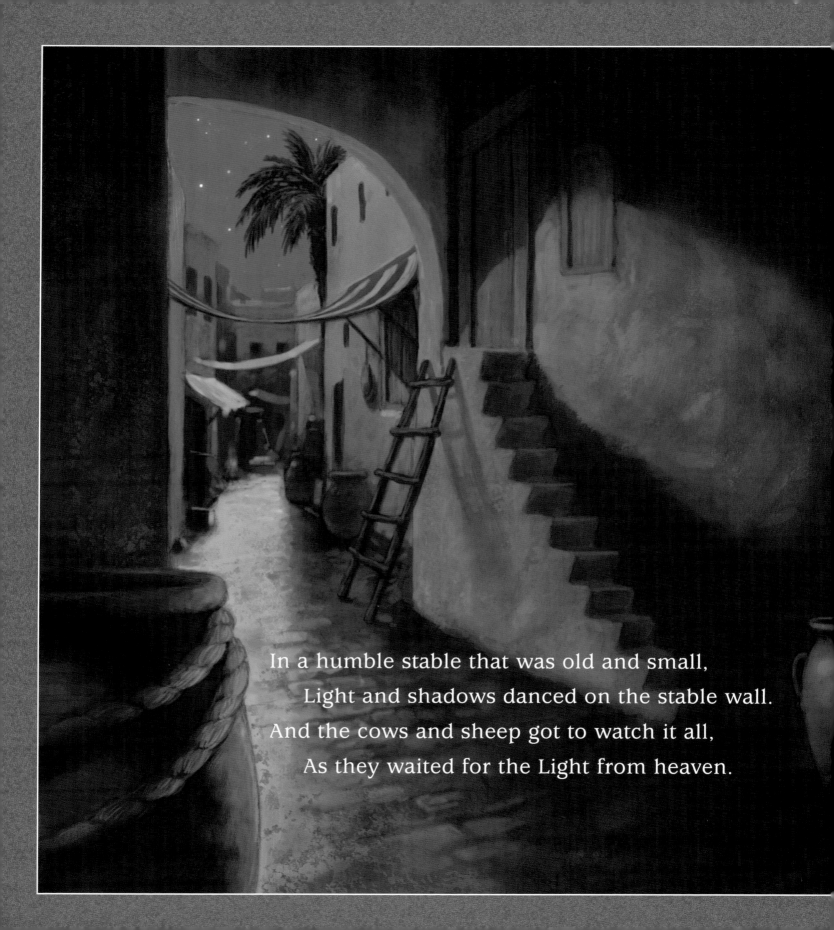

In a humble stable that was old and small,
  Light and shadows danced on the stable wall.
And the cows and sheep got to watch it all,
  As they waited for the Light from heaven.

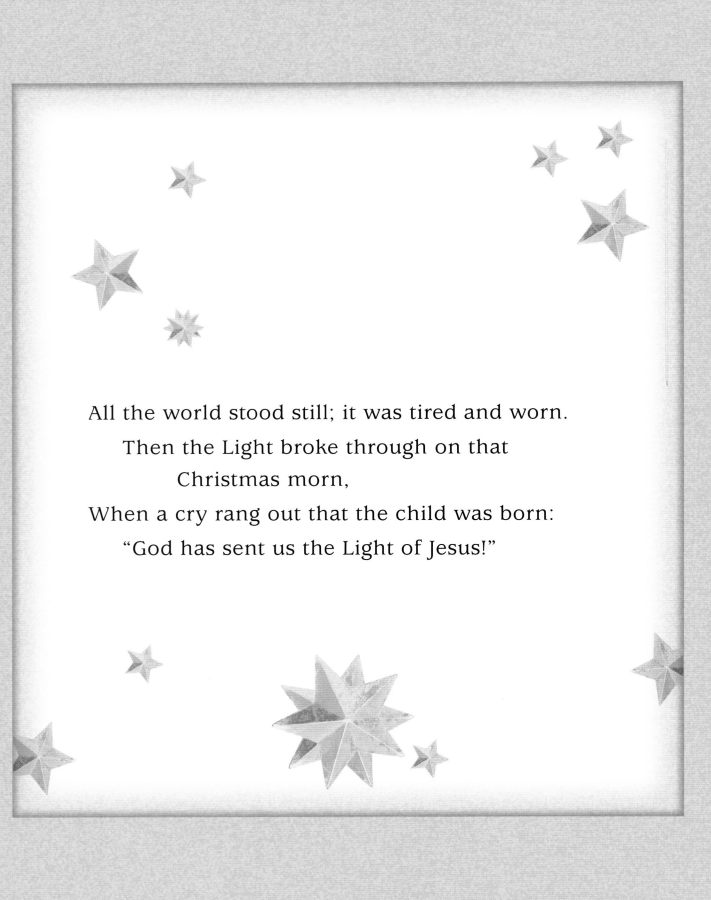

All the world stood still; it was tired and worn.
Then the Light broke through on that
Christmas morn,
When a cry rang out that the child was born:
"God has sent us the Light of Jesus!"

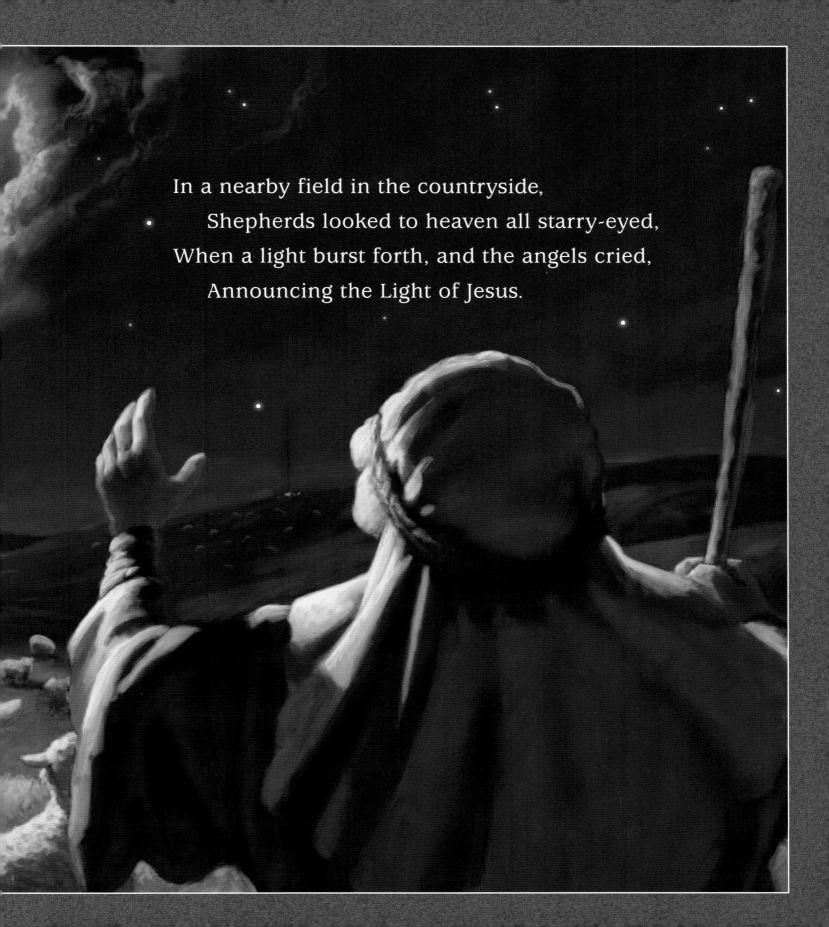

In a nearby field in the countryside,
Shepherds looked to heaven all starry-eyed,
When a light burst forth, and the angels cried,
Announcing the Light of Jesus.

In a far off land, there were three wise kings.
   "Let us follow the light that the bright star brings!"
So they rode on camels with gifts and things,
   Seeking the Light from heaven.

As the years went by, Jesus grew and grew.
  He obeyed the Lord and His parents, too,
Spreading love and light, making all things new.
  Jesus, the Light from heaven.

Jesus fed the crowds by the sun-splashed sea,
  Caused the deaf to hear and the blind to see.
And He showed the light of eternity.
  People walked in the Light of Jesus.

"I'm the Light of the world!" They heard His claim.
   "Come and follow Me! This is why I came."
But they loved the dark, and they cursed His name,
   And they hated the Light from heaven.

He was crucified on a cold, dark hill.
   And He died for us by His Father's will.
There was no more light. All was lost and still . . .
   We needed the Light of Jesus.

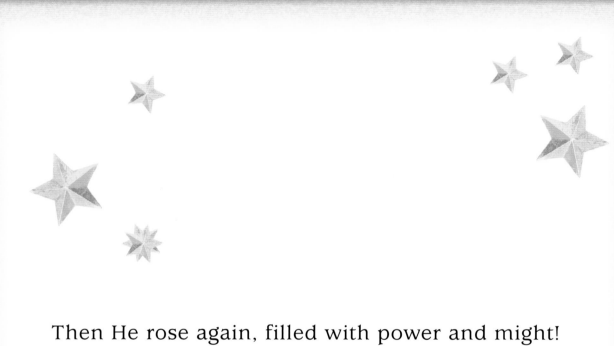

Then He rose again, filled with power and might!
And the world rejoiced at the wondrous sight.
All the earth was filled with His glorious Light,
The Light of the risen Savior!

So go ahead and trim that tree!
Light the lights for all to see!
Christ's light shines for you and me.
We still need the Light of Jesus.